12/98 B+T 21.36

WORD BIRD

ASKS: WHAT? WHAT? WHAT?

by Jane Belk Moncure
illustrated by Vera Gohman

THE CHILD'S WORLD

Library of Congress Cataloging in Publication Data

Moncure, Jane Belk.
   Word Bird asks: What? What? What?

   (Word Birds for early birds)
   Summary: Word Bird goes for a walk in the country
with his father and asks a lot of questions about what
he sees.
   [1. Birds-Fiction.   2. Questions and answers—
Fiction.   3. Vocabulary] I. Gohman, Vera Kennedy,
1922-   , ill. II. Title. III. Series: Moncure,
Jane Belk.   Word Birds for early birds.
PZ7.M739Wm   1983   [E]   83-15258
ISBN 0-89565-258-7

WORD BIRD

ASKS: WHAT? WHAT? WHAT?

One Saturday Word Bird
and Papa went for a walk.

They walked to a pond.
"What is in the pond?"
asked Word Bird.

"Let's find out,"
said Papa.

They found

frogs and

tadpoles and

6

ducks.

What else?

Then they walked in the woods.

"What is in the woods?"
asked Word Bird.

"Let's find out,"
said Papa.

They found

chipmunks,

acorns,

a raccoon

and

a little deer.

What else?

Word Bird and Papa
walked into a field.

"What is in the field?"
asked Word Bird.

"Let's find out," said Papa.

They found
daisies

and more
daisies.

They found
butterflies,

a bunny,

and
grasshoppers.

What else?

They came to a farm.

"What is on a farm?"
asked Word Bird.

"Let's find out," said Papa.

They found a cow
and a calf,

a hen,

a mother pig
and piglets,

sheep and

lambs.

What else?

Papa and Word Bird
walked down the road.

"What was that?" asked
Word Bird.

Then he saw Mama
in the truck.

"Let's have a picnic,"
she said.

"What is in the picnic basket?" asked Word Bird.

"Let's find out," said Papa.

They found peanut butter
sandwiches,

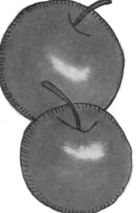

apples,

a pickle,

and carrot sticks.

MILK MILK

What else?

After the picnic, Word Bird asked, "What will we do now?"

"Let's go to the zoo,"
said Mama.

"What is in the zoo?"
asked Word Bird.

"Let's find out," said Papa.

They found monkeys…

a giraffe,

a camel,

and
polar bears.

What else?

"Let's get some ice cream," said Papa.

Word Bird did not ask,
What? What? What?
He knew just what
he wanted—

a
chocolate-
cherry-
vanilla-
strawberry-
ice cream
cone.

You can read these  words.

tadpole

pickle

chipmunk

calf

acorn

sandwich

daisy

basket

camel

grasshopper

raccoon

polar
bear

It's your turn to ask What? What? What?